"For Izzy."

- A.H. Benjamin

"For Roopsha.
Thanks for sticking by this camel
for as long as you have."

- Krishna Bala Shenoi

Get Off That Camel!

First Print January 2019

Author: A.H. Benjamin
Illustrator: Krishna Bala Shenoi

Karadi Tales Company Pvt. Ltd.
3A Dev Regency, 11 First Main Road,
Gandhinagar, Adyar, Chennai 600020
Tel: +91-44-42054243
email: contact@karaditales.com
www.karaditales.com

ISBN: 978-81-9390-331-5

Distributed in the United States by Consortium Book Sales & Distribution
www.cbsd.com

Cataloging - in - Publication information:

Printed and bound in India by Manipal Technologies Limited, Manipal

Benjamin, A.H.
Get Off That Camel / A.H. Benjamin; illustrated by Krishna Bala Shenoi
p.32; color illustrations; 24.5 x 24 cm.

JUV000000 JUVENILE FICTION / General
JUV002000 JUVENILE FICTION / Animals / General
JUV039060 JUVENILE FICTION / Social Themes / Friendship
JUV019000 JUVENILE FICTION / Humorous Stories

Get Off
That
Camel!

When Meena was a baby,
she had a cuddly toy camel.

She never slept without it.

When Meena was a toddler,
she had a rocking camel.

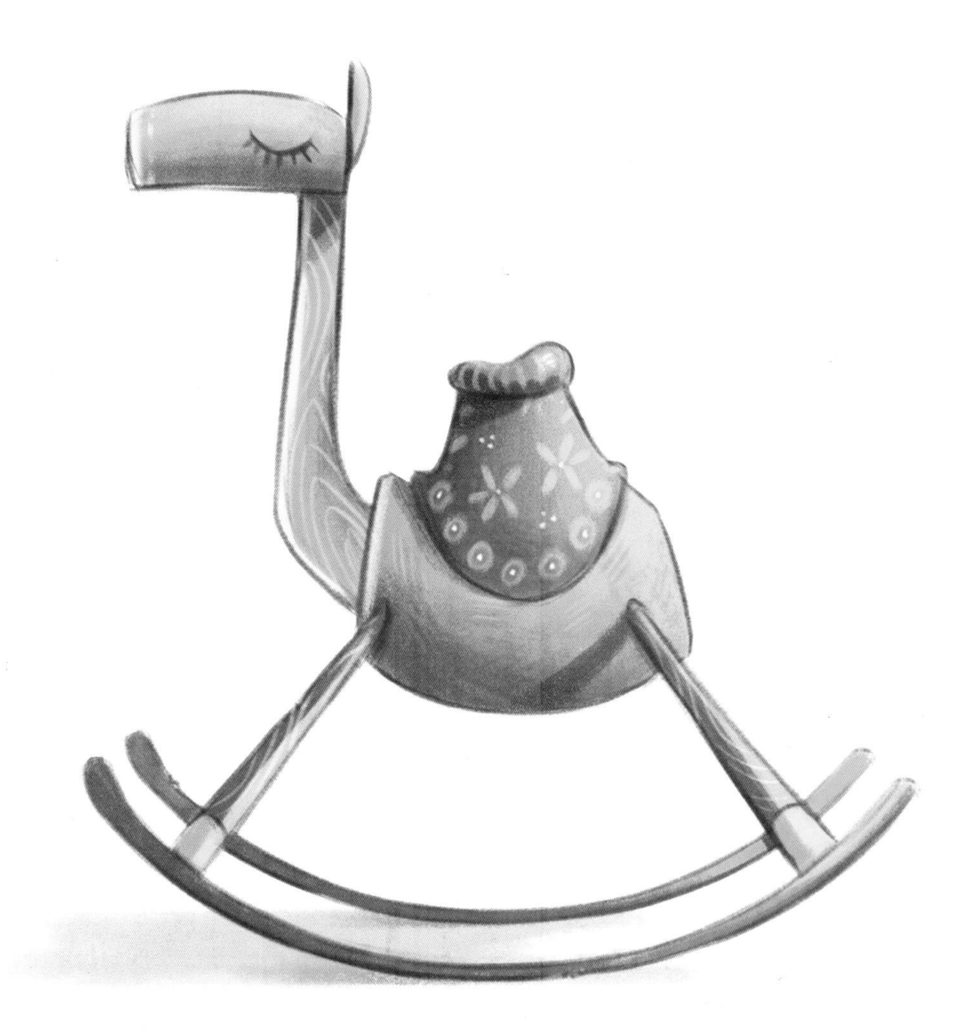

She never stopped
rocking on it.

When Meena was a bit older, she got...
a real camel!

“I’ll never get off her!” she said.
And she didn’t...

Not at the
dinner table...

Not in
the bath...

Not even at bedtime...

"Get off that camel!"

said Mum and Dad.
Meena didn't.

Meena got on the school bus.

"Get off that camel!" said the bus driver.

Meena didn't.

Meena sat at her desk.
Her classmates were not pleased.

"Get off that camel!" they yelled.

Meena didn't.

Meena helped Mum with the
shopping in the supermarket...

"Get off that camel!"
said the shop manager.

Meena didn't.

When Dad took her
jogging in the park...

"Get off that camel!" said the watchman.

Meena didn't.

Meena rode the camel everywhere.

“GET OFF THAT CAMEL!”

shouted everyone.
Meena didn’t.

Soon camels were not
allowed anywhere.

Yet, Meena refused to get off her camel.
Mum and Dad were worried.
They took her to see the doctor.

The doctor examined Meena and found nothing wrong with her.

"She's in perfect health!" he said. He then checked the camel.

"This poor animal is exhausted," he said.

Meena was quite a kind girl, really. "It's my fault," she said. "I'm always riding her."

She agreed to let her camel go and live in a stable. She would ride her only now and again.

A few weeks later, Mum and Dad had a surprise for Meena at home...

...a baby brother!

“He’s so cute!”
said Meena, delighted.
And she gave him her
old cuddly toy camel.

The baby loved his cuddly camel.
He never slept without it!

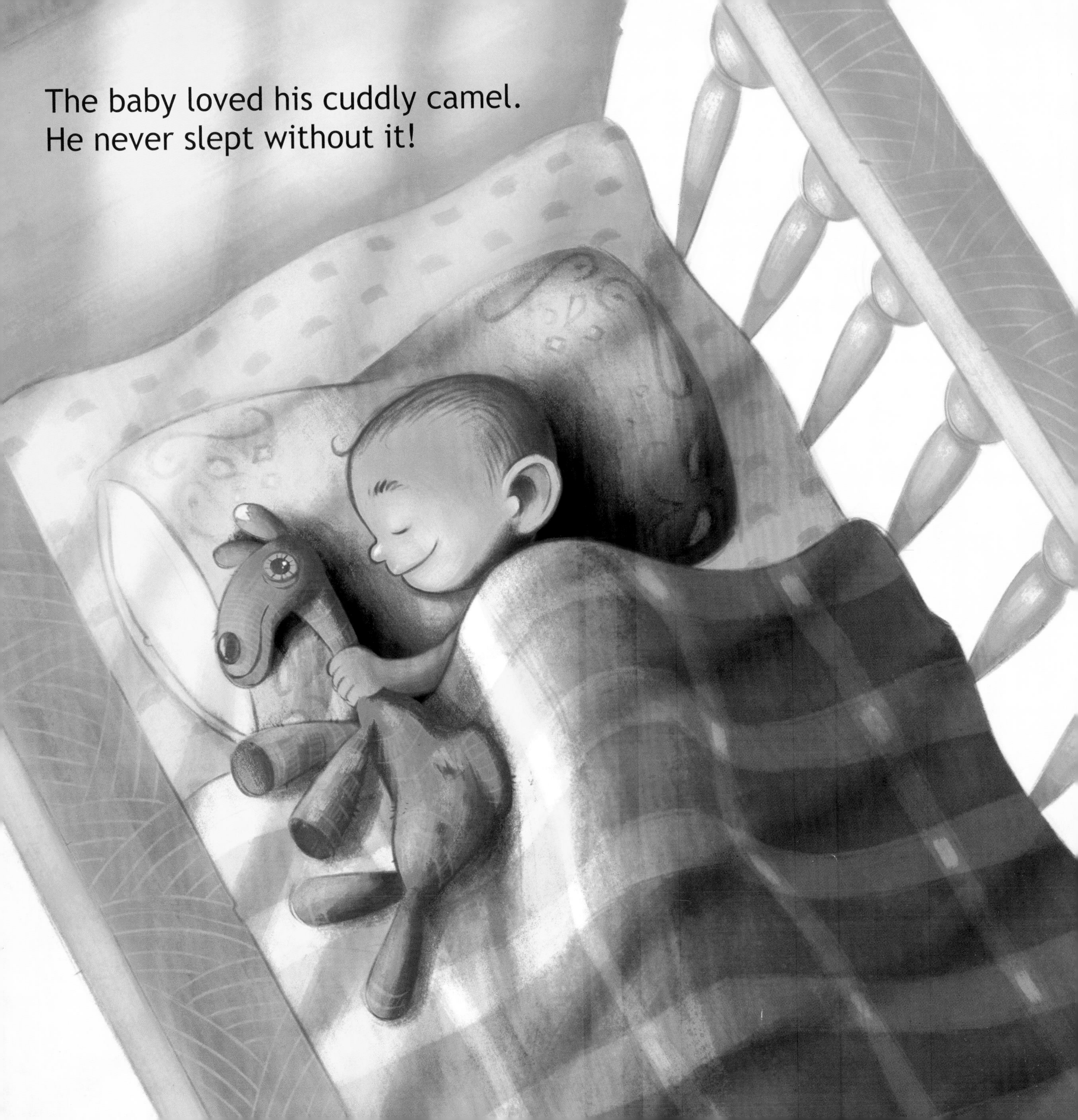

“Oh, no!”
said Mum and Dad.

FUN FACTS ABOUT CAMELS

- Camels have three eyelids! This is so they get protection from the desert sand

- A baby camel is called a calf

- A camel's hump has a very useful purpose – it stores fat and is a source of energy

- In 2014, the camel was declared the State Animal of Rajasthan

- An adult camel is really tall, measuring 7 feet at the hump

- Camels greet each other by blowing in each other's faces

- These majestic beings are commonly referred to as the ships of the desert

- Camels spit on people when they feel threatened or stressed!

- Camels can guzzle up to 150 litres of water in a matter of a few minutes

- Camels have a lifespan of between 40 and 50 years

- Camels are intelligent, loyal, have a great memory, and have been known to embrace their owners as a show of affection

Ever since the mid-eighties, A.H. Benjamin has been writing books. He has written over forty books for publishing houses around the world which are available in more than twenty-five languages including Chinese, Korean, Turkish, Afrikaans, Greek, and Arabic. Some of his work has been adapted for other mediums such as radio, television, and theatre.

Krishna Bala Shenoi spends his days making things. His artwork, spanning a variety of styles, has accompanied children's literature in books produced by esteemed publishing houses. He lives in Bangalore with his family of humans and cats, where he plans to continue contributing to children's storytelling, imbuing his work with gentleness and a sense of wonder.